IF I WERE IN CHARGE OF THE FARM

by Rebecca Maurer

illustrated by Ashley Roth

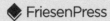 FriesenPress

One Printers Way
Altona, MB R0G 0B0
Canada

www.friesenpress.com

Copyright © 2022 by Rebecca Maurer
First Edition — 2022

ISBN
978-1-03-912952-8 (Hardcover)
978-1-03-912951-1 (Paperback)
978-1-03-912953-5 (eBook)

1. JUVENILE FICTION, LIFESTYLES, FARM & RANCH LIFE

Distributed to the trade by The Ingram Book Company

To all the kids, young and grown,
who love the farm.

This includes
Amy, Joel, Daniel and David.

The predator guard dogs that protect the goats and sheep would be able to **TAKE A BREAK** from their job.

vii

The farm cats would not be in trouble
if they **SUNTANNED** on the patio cushions.

If ▯ was in charge of the farm,
I would be the **BIG BOSS** of the sprinkling
hose. All the plants would grow while Grandma
could relax and drink her coffee.

If I were in charge of the farm, I would read my favourite books to put my Papa to sleep after lunch so he would not be

SO GRUMPY!

Being in charge of the farm, Mom would ask me to steer the **SIDE-BY-SIDE** out to the canola field to check for little **GREEN** worms.

Every day I would **RIDE** shotgun in the old farm truck with my Dad to **CHECK** the cows.

Badgers and gophers would be OUTLAWED on every farm field. No horse or cow would ever break a leg from one of their holes again.

xvii

As the Money trees **GROW**, I would carefully pick the paper money off the trees to pay for our farm expenses. I would pay cash to cover the feed bills for all my special animals.

If  were in charge of the farm,
my chickens would lay different kinds of eggs.
In the nests I would find
brown, white, coloured,
decorated and
my favourite...
**CHOCOLATE
EGGS!**

Everyone would be so happy that I was in charge of the farm, they would allow me to have all the animals I ever wanted to live on our farm.

About the Author

REBECCA MAURER is a first-time author. Working as a teacher for thirty years, her great passion was to instill the love of reading, and to encourage her students to be critical thinkers. She was inspired to write If I Were in Charge of the Farm as she witnessed her young grandchildren coming to understand the responsibilities of farm life.

Rebecca lives on a mixed farm in southern central Saskatchewan with her wonderful farmer, two farm dogs, and barnyard cats. She is the proud mother of four fantastic children, and grandmother of five fabulous grandchildren.

About the Illustrator

ASHLEY ROTH is Calgary based graphic designer, with a love for all things creative. She graduated from Montana State University Northern with a BA in Graphic Design and a minor in Design Drafting Technologies. She has worked in the print and design industry for 13 years and has been designing as a freelance graphic designer for her company Ashechodesigns since 2017.

Ashley is a born and raised Saskatchewan farm girl who loves animals and farm life. She was thrilled with the opportunity to create the illustrations for If I Were In Charge of The Farm.